Sam the Man & the Dragon Van Plan

Also by Frances O'Roark Dowell

Anybody Shining
Chicken Boy
Dovey Coe
Falling In
The Second Life of Abigail Walker
Shooting the Moon
Ten Miles Past Normal
Trouble the Water
Where I'd Like to Be

The Secret Language of Girls Trilogy
The Secret Language of Girls
The Kind of Friends We Used to Be
The Sound of Your Voice, Only Really Far Away

From the Highly Scientific Notebooks of
Phineas L. MacGuire
Phineas L. MacGuire . . . Blasts Off!
Phineas L. MacGuire . . . Erupts!
Phineas L. MacGuire . . . Gets Cooking!
Phineas L. MacGuire . . . Gets Slimed!

The Sam the Man series
#1: *Sam the Man & the Chicken Plan*
#2: *Sam the Man & the Rutabaga Plan*
#3: *Sam the Man & the Dragon Van Plan*
#4: *Sam the Man & the Secret Detective Club Plan*

SAM THE MAN 3:

SAM THE MAN

& the Dragon Van Plan

DISCARD

FRANCES O'ROARK DOWELL

Illustrated by **Amy June Bates**

A Caitlyn Dlouhy Book

Ⱥ **Atheneum Books for Young Readers**

atheneum New York London Toronto Sydney New Delhi

atheneum

ATHENEUM BOOKS FOR YOUNG READERS
An imprint of Simon & Schuster Children's Publishing Division
1230 Avenue of the Americas, New York, New York 10020
ATHENEUM BOOKS FOR YOUNG READERS is a registered trademark of Simon & Schuster, Inc. Atheneum logo is a trademark of Simon & Schuster, Inc.
For information about special discounts for bulk purchases, please contact Simon & Schuster Special Sales at 1-866-506-1949 or business@simonandschuster.com.
The Simon & Schuster Speakers Bureau can bring authors to your live event. For more information or to book an event, contact the Simon & Schuster Speakers Bureau at 1-866-248-3049 or visit our website at www.simonspeakers.com.
Also available in an Atheneum Books for Young Readers hardcover edition
Book design by Sonia Chaghatzbanian
The text for this book was set in New Century Schoolbook LT Std.
The illustrations for this book were rendered in pencil.
Manufactured in the United States of America
0119 MTN
First Atheneum Books for Young Readers paperback edition February 2019
10 9 8 7 6 5 4 3 2 1
The Library of Congress has cataloged the hardcover edition as follows:
Names: Dowell, Frances O'Roark, author. | Bates, Amy June, illustrator.
Title: Sam the Man & the dragon van plan / Frances O'Roark Dowell ; illustrated by Amy June Bates.
Other titles: Sam the Man and the dragon van plan
Description: First edition. | New York : Atheneum Books for Young Readers, 2018. | Series: Sam the Man ; 3 | "A Caitlyn Dlouhy Book." | Summary: "When the family minivan needs replacing, Sam has the perfect plan to turn the new car into a monster minivan, complete with a dragon painted on it. But first, Sam has to convince his family why a monster minivan is the best choice—not to mention learn how to paint a dragon!"— Provided by publisher.
Identifiers: LCCN 2017009501
ISBN 9781481440721 (hc) | ISBN 9781481440738 (pbk) |
ISBN 9781481440745 (eBook)
Subjects: | CYAC: Vans—Fiction. | Family life—Fiction. Classification: LCC PZ7.D75455 Sar 2018 | DDC [Fic]—dc23
LC record available at https://lccn.loc.gov/2017009501

For Robert-Bob Stockfish,
dear friend, beloved crank

—F. O. D.

To my trusty minivan,
the Grey Hippo—
Keep on Rollin'!

—A. J. B.

Sam the Man & the Dragon Van Plan

Chapter 1

The Monster Truck Plan

Sam Graham was a monster truck man. Every year he and his dad went to the Monster Truck Jam downtown. They cheered for trucks with names like "Master of Disaster" and "Big Dawg." Sam's dad made him put squishy orange earplugs in his ears, but he could still hear the roaring engines as the trucks raced across the arena.

Every year Sam asked his dad if they

could get a monster truck of their own, and every year his dad said, "Sorry, Sam the Man, we're sticking with our minivan."

Every year Sam pointed out that there was never a minivan jam at the downtown arena.

"You know what a monster truck would be great for?" Sam asked one morning at breakfast. "If there were a huge blizzard and you were out of milk, a monster truck would get you to the store."

"So would a snowplow," Sam's sister, Annabelle, pointed out. Annabelle was in sixth grade and always pointing out stuff to Sam, who was in second grade and was tired of people always pointing out stuff to him.

"A snowplow wouldn't be any good in

summer," Sam replied. "But you could take a monster truck camping. You could roll out your sleeping bags underneath it. It's like an automatic roof."

"But where would you put your camping gear when you were driving?" Annabelle asked.

"In the truck bed, of course!" Sam said, wondering how someone as smart as Annabelle could be so dumb.

"What if it rains?"

Sam rolled his eyes at his sister. "You get waterproof stuff for camping. Everybody knows that!"

Annabelle picked up the sports page. She looked like she was losing interest in the conversation. "What about the fact that it's illegal to drive monster trucks on regular streets?" she asked. "Wouldn't that be a problem?"

Sam stood up and carried his cereal bowl over to the kitchen sink. He was losing interest in this conversation too, especially because Annabelle didn't know what she was talking about.

If anyone would know about trucks, Sam thought as he put on his coat and hat, it would be Miss Louise, the school bus driver. A school bus was even bigger than a monster truck, although it wasn't as high up in the air, and it usually didn't have a scary monster face drawn on the hood. In fact, buses never had anything good painted on them. Sam could think of a million things you could paint on a school bus—dragon scales would be cool, and so would big, creepy eyes around the head-lights so that maybe the front of the bus looked like a really spooky jack-o'-lantern.

"Do you think Miss Louise has ever driven a monster truck?" Sam asked his friend Gavin as they waited at the bus stop. "I think she'd be good at it."

"Miss Louise would be an awesome monster truck driver!" Gavin agreed. "But once, I heard her say that she spends her weekends making cat videos. Did you know she has five cats?"

5

"I wonder if her cats like chickens?" Sam had a chicken named Helga who lived in a coop at his neighbor's house. Mrs. Kerner had five chickens, and Sam's friend Mr. Stockfish had one chicken, so there were seven chickens in all. Maybe Sam should start making chicken videos. He'd probably get famous and make lots of money, and then he could buy his own monster truck. He'd call it the Sammer Hammer Jammer, and he'd drive it all over town as soon as he got his driver's license.

"Monster trucks are legal to drive anywhere, right?" he asked Miss Louise when he was climbing up the steps of the bus.

"I don't know much about monster trucks," Miss Louise told him, "but I do know you can't drive them on streets or highways. They're too high off the ground, for one thing, and too dangerous. They're more likely to roll over than regular cars."

So the two things Sam liked best about monster trucks were what made his dream to drive one impossible?

After that, Sam was in a grumpy mood for the rest of the day. He was grumpy in math because they were doing subtraction. He was grumpy in PE because they did square dancing. He was grumpy at lunch because his dad put strawberry jam on his peanut butter sandwich instead of grape jelly. Sam hated strawberry jam.

He was still in a grumpy mood that afternoon when he got off the bus. He was looking forward to stomping across the kitchen floor and eating frozen waffles without even bothering to put them on a plate when he got home. Then he would go take Mr. Stockfish on their daily walk to visit the chickens. Mr. Stockfish was always grumpy, so he and Sam would get along better than ever.

But when Sam got to his house, something was weird. His family's blue minivan wasn't in the driveway, even though it was Tuesday, and his mom worked from home on Tuesdays. Maybe she had to go to the store. But usually when Sam's mom had to go to the store, she made sure to be back when Sam got off the bus.

The front door was unlocked. "Mom?" Sam called out as he walked inside. "Are you home?"

"In the kitchen," Sam's mom said. Her voice sounded sort of strange. Maybe she was in a grumpy mood too.

Sam found his mom sitting at the table, drinking a cup of tea that smelled like apples and cinnamon. Sam's mom only drank tea when she was trying to calm down or right after she talked to Aunt Karen on the phone.

"Did someone steal the minivan?" Sam asked. "Is that why you're drinking tea?"

"I wrecked the minivan," Sam's mom said. She sighed. "I hit a bus."

"A school bus?" Sam practically shouted. He thought his mom might go to jail for that.

"No, a city bus. I was changing lanes. . . ." Sam's mom stopped and rubbed her forehead. She looked like she had a headache. "It's a long story. Let's just say I wasn't paying close enough attention."

"Were you talking on your phone?"

Sam asked. "Because you always say it's stupid to talk on the phone when you're driving."

"No! I never talk on my phone in the car!" Sam's mom sounded like she couldn't believe Sam would even suggest such a thing. "I was . . . singing. And . . . dancing. Well, not exactly dancing—it was more like bouncing."

"Did that song about walking on sunshine come on the oldies station?" Sam asked.

His mom nodded. "It's very hard not to bounce to that song. And really, it's not like I ran into the bus. I just got very, very close to it. There was no damage done to the bus at all. The minivan, on the other hand . . ."

Sam's eyes widened. Would they have

to get a new car? His eyes opened even wider. Maybe they could get a really cool car this time, a car that didn't make Sam practically fall asleep from boredom every time he got into it.

"What's wrong with the minivan?" Sam asked, trying to sound like he was very concerned with the minivan's health and hoped it would get well soon. "Is it okay?"

"No, Sam, it's not," his mom said, and then she took another sip of her apple-cinnamon tea. "It was pretty old to begin with, and then with the damage, well, it would cost more to repair it than the van is worth. We're going to have to get a new one."

Yes! A new car! Maybe they could get a red car, or a yellow one; maybe one that sort of looked like a race car. Sam wouldn't

11

mind driving around town in a car that looked like a race car.

Wait a minute! Maybe instead of another minivan, they could get a monster truck, a small one that you could drive without getting a ticket! Sam wasn't sure if there was such a thing as a mini-monster truck, but there might be.

He knew he needed to be very careful. If Sam asked to get a monster truck—or even a mini–monster truck—while his mom was feeling sad and upset, she'd probably say no. He'd have to figure out the right way to make her see that a monster truck was the right choice for their family.

Sam would have to come up with the perfect monster-truck plan.

Chapter 2

Angry Chickens

"A monster truck? Are you crazy?"

Mr. Stockfish shook his head at Sam and patted his chicken, Leroy, on the head. "It's illegal to drive monster trucks on the road. Did you know that?"

"I know that, but I'm not talking about a monster truck," Sam said as he poured fresh water into the chickens' waterer. "I'm talking about a *mini*–monster truck."

"So you mean a pickup truck?"

Now Sam shook his head. "A pickup truck is too small. But I'm pretty sure you could get a mini–monster truck, one that has big wheels, but not so big that you could get a ticket. And pickup trucks don't have names, but mini–monster trucks do. Plus, you get to paint mini–monster trucks so they look like scary stuff. You know, monsters or animals with sharp teeth."

"Like Leroy here," Mr. Stockfish said, giving his chicken another pat on the head. "Only she's got a sharp beak instead of teeth. And she's mean when she doesn't get fed on time."

"Maybe not exactly like Leroy," Sam said. "More like dragons and growling dogs. Especially dragons because they're long enough to cover the whole truck

14

and they have flames coming out of their mouths. A dragon truck would be really cool."

Mr. Stockfish put Leroy down and stood up. This meant he was ready to go home. "How many people can fit in your mini–monster truck, Sam?"

Sam picked up Leroy and put her back in the coop with the rest of the chickens. "I don't know. Two? Maybe four. Some trucks have two rows of seats."

"Who will do most of the driving when you get this truck?"

"Me, when I get my driver's license," Sam said. "But until then, my mom."

"Do you think your mom will want to drive a truck with an angry chicken on it?" Mr. Stockfish asked.

"No, but there won't be an angry

chicken on the truck," Sam said, holding the backyard gate open for Mr. Stockfish. "It will be a monster truck, not a chicken truck."

Sam and Mr. Stockfish walked for a few minutes without saying anything. Even though he didn't want to, Sam started to think about the problems with mini–monster trucks. First of all, he wasn't exactly sure there *were* mini–monster trucks, unless you counted Hot Wheels. Sam had three Hot Wheels monster trucks, but they were only a couple of inches big, which was too mini to be any good.

Second of all, Sam's mom liked to say that minivans might be boring, but they had a lot of space. She was always driving the girls in Annabelle's scout troop on field trips, and once, when Grammy

16

and Pop were coming for a visit, Sam's mom dumped three laundry baskets full of stuff she didn't have time to put away in the back of the minivan. Another time, she stored ten cases of fund-raiser popcorn there.

Sam was pretty sure mini–monster trucks didn't have a lot of storage space, at least not inside storage space. And anything you stored in the bed of the truck would get wet.

But then Sam remembered another thing that his mom liked about the minivan. She said it made her feel tall because the seat was higher off the ground than in a regular car.

Monster trucks make you taller! Sam decided that was a good motto for his mini–monster-truck plan.

"Not everything about a mini–monster truck is great," he said now as they walked up the sidewalk to Mr. Stockfish's house. Sam thought he sounded very reasonable and grown-up. "But I think the good things are gooder than the bad things are bad."

"If that's the argument you're going to make to your mother, I think you need to find a better word than 'gooder,'" Mr. Stockfish said, pushing his front door open.

"You're probably right," Sam said, practicing his agreeableness. His mom liked it when Sam was agreeable.

"You might also want to find out what a monster truck costs," Mr. Stockfish added. "It might be more expensive than you think."

Then Mr. Stockfish slammed the door

closed. Mr. Stockfish always slammed the door closed, so Sam didn't take it personally.

Plus, he thought Mr. Stockfish had given him good advice. He would do some research, come up with a truck budget, and then very reasonably and agreeably tell his mom that their new car should be a mini–monster truck. He would give her a list of why she would love a mini–monster truck.

Number one, the list would begin, *you will feel six feet tall when you drive.*

Number two, you will be the coolest mom in town.

Number three?

Sam didn't know what number three would be.

But he knew just the person to ask.

19

Chapter 3

A New Plan

nnabelle was sitting at the computer playing her favorite game, Big City Build 3. Sam liked it because whenever an old building needed demolishing, Annabelle let Sam be the demolition man. The demolition man got to swing the wrecking ball that knocked everything down.

"Let me finish this round, and then I'll help you," Annabelle said when Sam asked her to look something up on her phone. "I'm waiting for the city council to approve the plans for my new skyscraper."

A minute later Annabelle pounded her fist on the desk. "Safety code issues? What do they mean 'safety code issues'?"

Then she took a deep breath, paused her game, and went over to sit next to Sam on the couch. "So what are we looking up?"

"Mini–monster trucks," Sam told her.

"You mean monster trucks, don't you?" Annabelle asked as she tapped on the search engine app.

"No, I mean mini–monster trucks," Sam said. "I want to know if they actually exist or if I just made the whole idea up."

Annabelle tapped again and then typed "mini–monster truck" into the search engine box. "Oh, they exist all right," she said after a few seconds. "And you can have one for a hundred thousand dollars."

"Is that more than what a regular car would cost?" Sam asked.

"It depends on the kind of car," Annabelle said. "But the kind of car our family would buy? Yes, it's a lot more. A lot, lot more."

"A lot, lot, *lot* more?"

Annabelle turned and looked at Sam. "Sam the Man, you know we're not getting a monster truck, a mini–monster truck, a garbage truck, or even a truck truck, right?"

"But I have a plan!" Sam told his sister.

"So do Mom and Dad," Annabelle informed him. "We're going out car shopping after dinner tonight. *Minivan* shopping."

Minivan shopping? Sam slumped over. Could there be two worse words in the English language?

"I like these mini–monster trucks, though," Annabelle said as she scrolled down a screen filled with images. "Look at this one—it's pink!"

"I think we should stop talking now," Sam said.

"I understand," Annabelle replied. "Want to go demolish a building before dinner?"

Sam nodded glumly. "Sure, but I don't think it will make me feel much better."

Annabelle stood up. "Look at it this way, Sam: Things can't get much worse, right? So they'll only get better."

"Dinner's almost ready!" their mom

called from the kitchen. "We're having beans!"

"Maybe they'll get better later," Annabelle said with a sigh.

Sam didn't bother answering. He was pretty sure things would never get better.

"Are you ready to go car shopping, Sam the Man?" Sam's dad asked as he passed Sam a bowl of rice. "You can help pick out the color! Don't you think that would be fun?"

Sam took a deep breath and let it out. He and his dad had very different ideas about what the word "fun" meant.

"Okay, Sam, what's wrong?" Sam's mom asked. "You've been acting strange all afternoon. Are you sad about the minivan getting wrecked?"

"Not really," Sam said. "It was pretty

old, and it smelled funny whenever it rained."

Sam's mom nodded. "I could never figure out what caused that."

"It's from when Sam threw up two years ago," Annabelle said. "You can never really get rid of that throw-up smell."

"Not exactly dinner-table talk, Annabelle," Sam's mom said.

"Not while I'm eating beans, please, Anna Banana," his dad said.

"What's wrong with beans?" Sam's mom asked his dad.

"When did you start calling me Anna Banana?" Annabelle asked Sam's dad.

Sam couldn't take it anymore. He stood up. He threw his napkin onto the table. "Minivans are boring!" he yelled. "Everybody knows it!"

"That's why we're getting another one, Sam the Man," his dad said. "Boring cars are safe cars."

"But I don't want a safe car," Sam said. "I want an exciting car."

"He wants a monster truck," Annabelle informed her parents.

"I want a mini–monster truck," Sam informed his parents. "It's smaller than a monster truck, and safer. You can drive it on the road."

He turned to his mother. "And you would feel very tall if you drove it."

Then Sam sat back down because he wasn't done eating his dinner.

"I'll tell you what we'll do, Sam the Man," his dad said. "We'll get a *red* mini-van. That sounds exciting, doesn't it?"

Sam closed his eyes. Why was he the

only reasonable person in his family?

"Sam?" his mom asked. "Do you feel okay?"

"Did you hear me, Sam?" his dad asked. "A red car will make us feel like we're going faster, even when we're driving the speed limit!"

Annabelle walked over to Sam's side of the table and kneeled beside him. "It's going to be okay, Sam. You'll come up with a plan."

Sam considered this. "You mean a monster-truck plan?"

"A monster-*something* plan," Annabelle said, patting Sam on the shoulder. "You're better at coming up with plans than anyone I know."

It was true, Sam thought, taking a bite of his now-cold beans that he didn't really hate. He was the best planner around. He might be the best planner in the universe.

And just like that, he knew what he was going to do.

He would come up with a monster-*minivan* plan.

Chapter 4

The Bow Tie Minivan Man

Sam's dad wanted to get a new minivan, but Sam's mom wanted to get a used minivan. Annabelle said she didn't care what kind of minivan they got, as long as the seats were covered in fake leopard skin.

Sam wanted to go home. There was something depressing about a big showroom full of shiny new minivans. They all looked alike, although the colors were different: silver, light blue, dark blue,

dark gray, and a strange brown color called "smoky topaz." None of the minivans had seats covered in fake leopard skin, so Annabelle lost interest in looking at them after five minutes.

Sam had never had any interest in the first place. Why were minivans so boring? They were like the brontosauruses of the car world.

The salesman was named Matt, and he was wearing a polka-dotted bow tie. "Even if folks don't remember my name, they remember my tie!" he told the Grahams when he introduced himself. Matt was very excited about a new line of minivans. "Nowadays, a minivan is like a house on wheels!" he said. "The Blu-ray player lets you experience movies like you were in your own living room!"

"No Blu-ray player," Sam's mom said.

"Our kids have enough screen time already," Sam's dad said.

"Then let's talk about the amazing in-dash satellite radio!" Matt said. "You're okay with music, right?"

"Music makes my mom bounce," Sam said. "So maybe it isn't a good idea."

Matt looked confused. Sam's mom put her hand on Sam's shoulder and squeezed. Hard. "Just a family joke," she told Matt. "But we don't need a fancy radio setup. Mostly we just listen to CDs."

"You know CDs are about to become a thing of the past, right?" Annabelle asked her mom. "Satellite and wireless are really your best options."

"She's absolutely right," Matt agreed. "Still, a CD player is part of the package.

32

In fact, there's no reason you can't get satellite, wireless, and a CD player!"

Sam's mom looked at Sam's dad. "I really think we should consider getting a used van," she said. "These new minivans are making me nervous."

"You'd probably feel pretty bad if you wrecked a new minivan," Sam agreed. "But if you wrecked an old one, who cares?"

Sam's mom looked like she couldn't decide whether to laugh or cry. "I think I just wrecked an old minivan this morning," she said. "But it's important to take care of your car, whether it's old or new."

"That's right, Sam the Man," his dad said. "A used car is just a new car with a few more miles on it. If you take care of it, it will take care of you."

Annabelle had been tapping away on her phone. Now she held it up. "There are a ton of used minivans for sale online, Mom. A lot of them look almost new."

Matt's smile looked like it was about to turn into a frown. "A new-model minivan is going to have safety features that an old one doesn't," he said. "That's something to think about."

"I think we should think about it over ice cream," Sam's mom said. "Let's go to Smiley's and discuss."

"Matt too?" Sam asked, hoping the answer was no. Matt was nice, but his tie was starting to get on Sam's nerves.

"I think Matt is on the job right now," Sam's dad said. "But we appreciate how helpful he's been."

"Happy to be of service!" Matt said,

although he didn't sound happy at all. "Come back anytime. Remember, I'm the guy with the tie!"

"How could we ever forget?" Annabelle muttered as they turned to head to the door.

"Don't be rude, Annabelle," Sam's mom said.

"He's just doing his job, Anna Banana," his dad said.

"I don't think the Anna Banana thing is working out, Dad," Annabelle said.

"Can I have two scoops of chocolate-Oreo-mint in a waffle cone with whipped cream and sprinkles and M&Ms?" Sam asked.

"We'll see, Sam the Man," his mom said.

Sam knew that meant the answer was

no. But he also knew that now he could ask for one scoop plus whipped cream and sprinkles, and his mom would think he was being very reasonable and mature and say yes.

At least that was the plan.

When they got home from Smiley's Ice Cream Shop, it was almost Sam's bedtime. His mom said he could play in his room for fifteen minutes after he put on his pajamas and brushed his teeth, but Sam decided to draw instead of play. He put the minivan brochure Matt had given them at the car dealership on his desk and copied the minivan shape onto a sheet of paper. He drew the windshield and the windows and the doors. He drew the tires.

"I think a used minivan would be good

because we wouldn't worry if it got a little bit scratched," Sam had said when they were at Smiley's.

"Or if somebody bumped into it in the grocery store parking lot," Annabelle had added.

Sam knew why Annabelle wanted a used minivan. If they got a used minivan, she could buy fake leopard-skin material at the craft store and cover the seats with it.

But what Annabelle didn't know is that Sam wanted a used minivan because then his mom would let him paint it. Well, he was pretty sure she would let him paint it. She was always saying she wanted Sam to spend more time on arts and crafts and less time on the computer, wasn't she?

Sam began to draw dragon scales on

the side of the minivan in his picture. He wasn't sure if he was getting them exactly right. He stood up and walked across the hall to Annabelle's room.

"Do you have any pictures of real dragons I could look at?" he asked when Annabelle opened her door.

"I have the best dragon book ever," she said. "But you have to promise to be very careful with it, because it's the only one in the world."

Annabelle went over to the wicker trunk at the end of her bed, opened it, and pulled out a folder. "I made this book in fourth grade," she told Sam, opening the folder. "I've always meant to get it published, but I haven't had the time."

Inside the folder was a homemade book. It had a cover and was held together by purple yarn that Annabelle had poked through punched-out holes and then tied. On the front cover was a picture of a fire-breathing dragon wearing a gold crown. *Kings + Queens of the Dragon World in Alphabetical Order* was written underneath.

"You may check it out of my room for twenty-four hours," Annabelle said. "But you have to keep it in the folder when you're not looking at it, and you have to wash your hands before you touch it."

Sam nodded. "I promise," he said, taking the folder from Annabelle. "And I'll give it back to you by eight thirty tomorrow night."

"Let's make that eight, just to be on the safe side," Annabelle said.

"Okay," Sam agreed.

KINGS + QUEENS
of the Dragon World
in
alphabetical order
by Annabelle Graham

He took the folder back to his room and carefully put it on his desk. Then he went to wash his hands. When he returned he opened up the book and looked at Annabelle's pictures. It wasn't until page fourteen when he found exactly the right one.

The dragon on page fourteen had a long tail and silvery green scales that looked like the letter *C* drawn over and over again.

Sam knew these were exactly the right sort of dragon scales for his monster minivan.

No, for his *family's* monster minivan. Their dragon van.

Sam smiled and began to draw. He couldn't wait to show his mom and dad first thing in the morning.

They were going to love his dragon-minivan plan.

Chapter 5

Dragon Tales

"Here's a white one that's used but really nice," Sam's mom said when Sam walked into the kitchen the next morning. She was standing at the counter, drinking coffee and looking at her laptop. Sam could see a picture of a shiny white minivan on the screen. "But white gets so dirty, especially in the winter."

"White would be good if you ever wanted to paint it another color," Sam pointed out. He pulled a box of cereal from the cupboard. "Maybe even more than one color."

"We could paint a rainbow on it," Sam's mom said with a laugh. "We'd have the most cheerful minivan in town."

Not in a million years, Sam thought, cringing on the inside.

But what he said was, "Rainbows are nice."

As he poured cereal into a bowl, Sam thought about showing his mom his monster minivan picture, but then decided to wait. For one thing, he wasn't finished coloring it in yet. For another thing, he had just planted the idea of painting the van in his mom's brain. Maybe he should give it time to grow.

"Your dad and I are taking the morning off from work to go look at some used minivans," Sam's mom said. "Maybe we'll have a new car by the time you get home from school."

"A new used car?" Sam asked, pouring milk over his cereal.

"A new-to-us used car," his mom said. "I wonder—once we drive it, does it become a used used car?"

"Now I'm confused," Sam said.

"Me too," his mom said.

When Sam finished breakfast, he went upstairs to get his backpack. He decided to take his monster minivan picture with him to school so he could finish it during lunch. He looked at Annabelle's book, which was open on his desk. Maybe he should take it too, just in case he needed inspiration.

Sam put the book back in its folder and put the folder in his backpack. A small voice in his head told him he should probably ask Annabelle's permission. But if he took the time to ask Annabelle's permission, then he might miss the bus, and if he missed the bus, then his parents would have to drive him to school, and if his parents drove him to school, they might not have time to look at the used but new-to-them white minivan.

If his parents didn't buy the white minivan, then how could Sam turn it into a monster minivan?

If he asked Annabelle's permission and he missed the bus and his parents had to drive him and then didn't buy the white minivan, Sam's plan for the dragon monster minivan would be ruined!

So he guessed he wouldn't ask. He'd just be very careful.

"If I show you something, can you keep it a secret?" he asked Gavin on the bus. "I mean, you can't tell anyone, okay?"

"I am the best secret keeper in the universe," Gavin exclaimed. "You can trust me."

"How about that time when I told you

that I was going to be a football for Halloween, only it was a secret and you told the whole class?"

"That was last year," Gavin said. "First grade was different. I was a different person."

Sam guessed this was true. In first grade Gavin wore the same pair of socks every day for three weeks. Now he changed his socks once a week, whether he needed to or not.

Sam pulled out his drawing from his backpack along with Annabelle's folder. "We're getting a new minivan, and I get to paint it to look like a dragon," he told Gavin.

"Your mom and dad said you could?" Gavin's eyes got wide.

"It's going to be a used minivan," Sam

explained without actually answering Gavin's question. "So it's okay to paint on it."

"A dragon would be really cool!" Gavin said. "Will it be a fire-breathing dragon?"

"Of course," Sam said. "Here, look at my picture. It's not done yet, but you'll get the idea."

Gavin looked at Sam's picture. "That looks like a real dragon!"

Sam nodded, feeling proud. "It took me twenty minutes to draw. I used Annabelle's book for ideas. You can look at the book, if you're very, very careful."

Gavin took the book from Sam. "'*Kings + Queens of the Dragon World in Alphabetical Order*,'" he read out loud. "Wow, that's a good title. I didn't know dragons even had kings and queens."

"Yeah, you can learn a lot reading that book," Sam said. "It's got a bunch of interesting facts in it."

"You should ask Mr. Pell to read it to the class after lunch," Gavin said.

Sam thought that was a good idea. After Mr. Pell read Annabelle's book, Sam could show everyone his picture

of the dragon monster minivan.

"So what was the secret again?" Gavin asked.

"That my parents are probably going to let me paint our new van," Sam said. "It's a secret because once everyone finds out, they'll start bugging their parents to paint their minivans, and then their parents will call my parents to complain. . . ."

"And your parents might change their minds if everyone is bugging them about it," Gavin said. "I totally get that."

"I guess another secret is that I didn't exactly ask to bring Annabelle's book to school." Sam's stomach hurt a little bit thinking about this. He knew that Annabelle expected him to be very careful with her book.

"Do you think she'd be mad if she knew?" Gavin asked.

"She made me check it out of her room."

"Like her room was a library?"

Sam nodded. "Yeah. I have to turn it back in by eight tonight."

Gavin handed the book back to Sam. He looked like he thought Annabelle needed to chill out. "You better be careful with it, I guess."

"That's the plan," said Sam. He put Annabelle's book back in its folder, and then he put the folder back in his backpack. He had to push a little to get it to fit between his math book and his spelling book. He tried not to push too hard though, because he didn't want any of the pages to—

Riiiip.

"What was that?" Gavin asked. "Did someone just fart?"

Sam squinched his eyes closed. He pulled the folder back out of his backpack.

"That doesn't look too good, Sam," Gavin said. "It looks like you just put Annabelle's book in the garbage disposal."

Sam opened his eyes. The cover of the folder was scrunched. The cover of the book was pinched, like someone had tried to fold it into a fan. He could see that the first few pages of the book were torn.

"That looks really bad," Sam said. "Really, really bad."

"But just on the outside," Gavin said. "Which, okay, is a really important side. Maybe more important than the inside, but maybe not."

"Thanks," Sam said, feeling like he'd

just swallowed a box of rocks. "That makes me feel better."

"I don't think anything is going to make you feel better," Gavin said. "Not unless you figure out how to fix it."

Sam stared at the torn cover. He couldn't fix it—not with tape, not with glue, not with staples. It was unfixable. Annabelle would never let him borrow anything of hers again.

"Hey!" Gavin exclaimed, punching Sam in the shoulder. "I bet I know who can help us!"

Sam felt better when Gavin said the word "us." It made him feel like he wasn't alone. "Who can help?" he asked.

"Miss Fran will come to our rescue," Gavin said with a big grin.

Miss Fran was their art teacher. At

the beginning of the school year she had purple hair. Now it was blue. She didn't look like the sort of grown-up who could help you with a problem, but Miss Fran was smart. Whenever they had an assembly in the gym, someone always went to get Miss Fran to run the A/V equipment. She also fixed the toilet in the girls' bathroom once.

The Miss Fran Will Help Us Fix the Book plan. Sam liked it.

He just hoped it would work.

Chapter 6

Just a Dab Will Do Ya

When it was time for recess, Sam and Gavin went to the art room. Miss Fran was always in the art room, no matter what time of day it was. A lot of people said she lived there, like the art room was her apartment. If that was true, Sam wondered if her husband lived there too.

"Sam! Gavin!" Miss Fran called when she saw them. She was sitting at the long table in the back of the room, cutting something out with her very sharp scissors that nobody else was allowed to touch. "Not even the principal can use these scissors!" Miss Fran always said, which made everybody happy. Miss Fran's students liked the idea that the principal had to follow the same rules they did.

"What are you doing?" Gavin asked. "Are you making snowflakes? Because I'm really good at cutting out snowflakes."

"I'm making silhouettes for my classroom windows," Miss Fran explained. "Right now I'm working on a swing set and some monkey bars. When I'm done I'll have an entire playground."

She held up a piece of black paper with a lot of pieces cut out. When Sam looked closer he could see a swing going up in the air. "That looks real!" he said. "I mean it would look real if swings were made out of black construction paper."

"Thanks, Sam!" Miss Fran said. "I'm glad you like it. Now, are you guys here to work on your art projects?"

"We're here because we're in trouble," Gavin told her. He lowered his voice. "Big trouble."

"Did you rob a bank?" Miss Fran asked.

"Worse," said Sam, taking Annabelle's torn book out of its scrunched folder. "I wrecked Annabelle's book."

"Annabelle's his sister," Gavin explained. "She's in sixth grade. She's not mean or anything, but this is going to make her mad."

Miss Fran took the book from Sam and nodded. "It's a cool book. Your sister is a good artist. What did you do, Sam, try to stuff it in your backpack?"

Sam nodded glumly. "I pushed too hard."

"It happens," Miss Fran said. "The bad news is, we can't make it look like nothing ever happened to it."

Sam stared at the floor. Just like he thought—the book was ruined.

"But we can do some repairs," Miss Fran said. "We can make it look almost as good as new."

"Maybe Annabelle won't even notice!" Gavin said. "That would be so awesome!"

Miss Fran looked at Sam. "I think you ought to tell her, don't you, Sam?"

Sam didn't think that at all. What he thought was that after they repaired the book, he should sneak it back into Annabelle's wicker trunk and hope that she never looked at it or asked about it again.

"Sam?" Miss Fran was still looking at Sam, only now her look was a question that said, *You're going to do the right thing, aren't you?*

Sam sighed. Sometimes he hated doing the right thing. "I guess so," he told Miss Fran.

"Okay, then, let's get started!"

Miss Fran put the pieces of her silhouette project in a large plastic envelope to make room for the three of them to work. "What we'll need is some glue, some water, and a paintbrush," she told Sam and Gavin. She handed Gavin a small plastic cup. "Can you fill this up at the sink, please? And can you please not splash water on the paintings that are drying on the counter next to the sink?"

Gavin looked insulted. "I am the most careful person in the universe," he said. "I never splash."

Miss Fran turned to Sam. "Your job is to put some glue into this dish."

Sam squeezed some white glue onto the blue dish Miss Fran put in front of him. When Gavin gave Miss Fran the cup of water, she poured a little bit into the dish and then mixed it up with a paintbrush. Then she poured in a little more and mixed a little more.

"I'm thinning the glue," she explained. "If you get too much glue on the paper, it's going to get all gunky, if you know what I mean."

Sam and Gavin nodded. They knew exactly what she meant.

"Good," Miss Fran said. "Okay, I think

we're ready to start. First we're going to remove the yarn that's holding the book together so we can work on the torn pages one by one." She handed Sam a pair of scissors. They weren't her very sharp scissors, but they still looked pretty sharp to Sam. "I don't think we can pull out the yarn without tearing the cover even more, so we're going to clip it. You up for the job, Sam?"

"I think so," Sam said. He snipped the first piece of yarn, careful not to cut the cover. It worked! He pulled out the yarn and then cut the second piece and the third and fourth pieces and pulled them out too.

"Well done!" Miss Fran said. "Now that we've freed the cover, I'm going to put it under that pile of art books over there.

We'll see if we can't press those crinkles out."

"Do you think we can?" Sam asked hopefully.

Miss Fran carried the cover over to the windowsill. "It's not going to be perfect, Sam. But we can make it better."

Better was okay, Sam guessed. But would it be good enough?

"Now on to the glue!" Miss Fran said when she returned to the table. "I'll be in charge of this part, if that's okay with you guys."

"It's okay with me," Sam said.

"I guess it's okay," Gavin said. "Although I am an excellent gluer."

"I'm well aware of that," Miss Fran said. "But this is a special process." She held up page one of the book. "When you look closely, can you see that the torn parts of the paper are a little fuzzy? That's the paper fiber. What I'm going to do is paint a very light layer of glue on the bottom fuzzy part, and then I'll press the top part down onto the bottom part. With any luck the fibers will stick back together so that you can't see the tear anymore."

"Wow, it looks perfect!" Gavin said when Miss Fran finished. "I want to learn how to do that!"

"You just did," Miss Fran said. She turned to Sam. "You know what, Sam? Why don't you do the next page?"

"I don't think so," said Sam. "I don't want to mess it up."

"You won't," Miss Fran said. "And maybe if you help repair Annabelle's book, you might not feel so bad about tearing it."

64

Maybe, Sam thought. But maybe not. Still, he could tell from looking at Miss Fran that she wasn't going to let him say no.

"Start with just a dab of glue, Sam," Miss Fran said when he picked up the brush. "Get a feel for how it feels, if you know what I mean."

Sam didn't know what she meant.

"This paper is art paper, so it will feel different than painting glue onto regular white paper. It's not as smooth."

Miss Fran was right. The paper felt rough. It felt like it wanted to stop the paintbrush from painting glue on it. Sam had already learned his lesson about pushing too hard, though, so he pretended the paintbrush was a feather he was dusting the paper with.

"That's right, Sam," Miss Fran said. "Nice and easy."

When Sam finished painting on the glue, he pushed the top fuzzy part down onto the bottom fuzzy part. When he took his finger away, he could hardly see where the tear was.

"It worked!" he said. "I fixed the tear!"

"High-five, Sam the Man," Gavin said. "You're a genius!"

Sam high-fived Gavin, and then he high-fived Miss Fran.

"Come back at lunch, Sam," she told him. "You can finish the other pages then."

"Could I come with him?" Gavin asked. "I'd like to tear up some sheets of paper and glue them back together."

"I'll find you some scrap paper," Miss Fran told him.

Sam and Gavin walked back to Mr. Pell's classroom. "I like a teacher who lets you tear stuff up," Gavin said.

"I like a teacher who helps you glue stuff back together," Sam said.

"Yeah, that's a good kind of teacher to have," Gavin agreed.

"Yeah," Sam said. "I'm pretty sure it's the best."

Chapter 7

No Bad News Is Good News

"What's the best way to give somebody bad news?" Sam asked Mr. Stockfish that afternoon as they walked over to Mrs. Kerner's house.

"What kind of bad news?" Mr. Stockfish asked.

"Say someone let you borrow something really important to them, and you sort of messed it up," Sam said. "That kind of bad news."

"I see," Mr. Stockfish said. "You mean the kind of bad news that's going to get you in trouble."

"Or at least make Annabelle really, really mad at me," Sam agreed.

Mr. Stockfish's eyes widened. "Bad news that makes Annabelle mad is very bad news indeed."

"I know," Sam said glumly. "Maybe I shouldn't tell her. She might never find out."

"But you'd know," Mr. Stockfish said. "What did you mess up?"

"A book that Annabelle made about dragons. I fixed it, so she might not even notice that I squished the cover and tore some of the pages."

"Still, *you'd* know," Mr. Stockfish repeated.

Boy, everybody seemed to think that he'd feel bad if he didn't tell Annabelle the truth. But Sam wondered if that was really true. He'd kept other secrets from his sister and felt okay. For instance, Sam had never told Annabelle that he'd accidentally flushed her green frog eraser down the toilet. He hadn't meant to. He just wanted to see it go round and round. Somehow he thought the eraser would bounce out before it went down the hole.

It hadn't.

As far as Sam knew, Annabelle never noticed her frog eraser was missing. Did he feel bad about flushing the frog down the toilet? Yes. Did he feel bad that Annabelle didn't know that he'd flushed it down the toilet? Not really, no.

So why did he need to tell Annabelle about the book if she might never notice something was wrong with it?

Still, if she *did* notice, he needed to have a plan. "You haven't told me the best way to give somebody bad news," Sam said as he and Mr. Stockfish reached Mrs. Kerner's backyard. "In case I decide to tell Annabelle about her book."

"You should tell her, Sam," Mr. Stockfish said, opening the backyard gate. "Honesty is the best policy."

"Maybe," Sam said. "But what's the best way to be honest?"

"Let me think about it," Mr. Stockfish said. "Spending time with the chickens always helps me think better."

When they reached the backyard, they found Mrs. Kerner sitting in one of the lawn chairs by the chicken coop. "Hello there!" she called. "Sam, I hear you're getting a new car!"

"Actually, we're getting an old car. My dad says we can use it to take the chickens to the vet if we need to," Sam said as he opened up the coop to let the chickens out. "It's a used new van so it's okay if it gets some feathers in it."

"Maybe you could paint feathers on the outside of the van," Mr. Stockfish said. He sat down in a lawn chair and settled Leroy on his lap. "The entire van could have a chicken theme."

"I think a dragon theme would be better," Sam said. "I'm working on a design. Did you know that before birds were birds, they were dragons? I mean, like a million years ago."

"I believe that before birds were birds, they were dinosaurs," Mrs. Kerner corrected Sam. "Not dragons."

"That doesn't make any sense," Sam said.

Mr. Stockfish cleared his throat. "Sam, you know that dragons are make-believe, don't you?"

"I'm pretty sure they were real," Sam said. "They came after the dinosaurs,

but before dragonflies. And birds."

"What's real is this chicken," Mr. Stockfish said, patting Leroy's tail feathers. "And a chicken, being a bird, has its origins in theropod dinosaurs. Do you know what the word 'theropod' means?"

Sam shook his head.

"'Bird foot,'" Mr. Stockfish said. "Well, some say it means 'beast foot,' but I beg

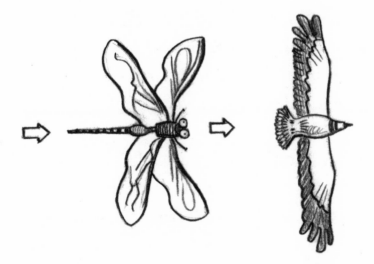

to differ. Look it up when you get home. And look up dragons, too."

"It's going to be bad news when I look up dragons, isn't it?" Sam asked, slumping into the chair next to Mr. Stockfish.

"Only if you believe dragons are real," Mr. Stockfish said.

"This has been a bad-news kind of day," Sam said. "First, Annabelle's book, and now fake dragons."

"But you repaired Annabelle's book so it's almost good as new," Mr. Stockfish pointed out. "Which is good news."

Maybe, Sam thought. Except almost good as new wasn't good enough.

"Hey, Sam!" Sam's dad called from the driveway when Sam got back from dropping off Mr. Stockfish. He was standing next to a very clean, very white minivan. "What do you think of our almost new, sort-of-used van?"

The first thing Sam noticed was that the Grahams' new-used white minivan looked a lot like a delivery truck, which wasn't nearly as good as looking like a monster truck or even a mini–monster truck, but at least it was better than looking like a plain old minivan.

The second thing he noticed was that this white minivan needed some serious decorating, just like he'd thought it would.

Sam bet his parents had noticed that too. Still, he thought he should drop a few hints when his dad opened up the minivan doors so Sam could see inside.

"It's nice in here," Sam told his dad.

"But I bet it will look even nicer when Annabelle covers the seats with leopard skin. Maybe we can spiff up the outside, too."

"I always thought 'spiff' was a funny word," Sam's dad said as he rubbed at a smudge on the dashboard. "What does it mean, exactly?"

Sam shrugged. "I think it means to make something a little more . . . well, a little more exciting, a little more fun to look at, in a nice way."

"Never a bad idea, Sam the Man," his dad said.

Sam wished that Gavin had been there to high-five. It was only a matter of time before his monster dragon van dreams came true.

A school bus pulled up in front of

their house. Annabelle! What if the first thing she did when she saw Sam was ask about her book? Sam popped out of the van, deciding he'd better take charge of this situation.

"Look at our new car!" Sam called out as soon as his sister stepped off the bus. "It's white!"

"I can see that, Sam," Annabelle said, rolling her eyes like she thought Sam was acting weird.

"I'm not acting weird," Sam blurted out. "I'm just excited about our new minivan!"

Annabelle stared at him. "Did I say you were acting weird?"

"Hey, Anna Bana—Belle," Sam's dad said. "Come look at the new car. Even though it's used, it actually has that new-car smell. There's a spray for that. Climb inside and you'll see."

Dad to the rescue! Sam leaned back against the side of the minivan, relieved. He'd almost blown his cover. Was it going to be like this for the rest of his life? Would he spend every day trying to keep Annabelle from asking about her book or looking at it too closely?

Maybe he should just tell her. It might be easier than being nervous about it all the time. But if he told her, he had to do it the right way. What had Mrs. Kerner said this afternoon when they'd talked about the best way to give bad news? Oh yeah—that you should always give a present. She said that if Sam had to give her bad news, he should give her a box of chocolate, too.

"I like a steak," Mr. Stockfish had said. "Medium rare, with a baked potato and green beans. But don't overcook the green beans, or that will make the bad news even worse."

Sam thought about this now. He guessed Annabelle liked chocolate, but she liked other things better, like computer games and goats. Sam couldn't afford a computer game, and his parents had said Annabelle couldn't have a goat until she bought her own house. Too bad Sam couldn't afford to buy Annabelle a house. Or—even better—a pink monster truck!

Sam knew Annabelle would forgive him if he said he was really, really sorry and then handed her the keys to a pink monster truck.

81

But he couldn't afford that either.

Sam sighed. And then his eyes opened wide. Wait a minute!

He didn't need to buy a monster truck.

All he needed was some pink paint.

Chapter 8

An Impractical Plan

"What's the best way to paint metal?" Sam asked his dad at dinner. "Like if you wanted to paint a car?"

"I'm pretty sure acrylic paint is best," Sam's dad said.

"You're not thinking about painting the car, are you?" Sam's mom asked. She sounded worried. "I know the new van has a scratch or two on it, but I sort of prefer it that way."

"In case you hit another bus," Annabelle said agreeably.

Their mom's cheeks turned pink. "Yes, Annabelle. In case I hit another bus. Which I won't."

"The thing I'm painting is a surprise so I can't say what it is," Sam said. He turned to his dad. "Do you have any acrylic paint I could use?"

"I'm afraid I don't, Sam the Man," his dad said. "But we could take a ride to the store after dinner, give the old minivan a spin."

"You mean the new minivan," his mom said.

"Or the new used minivan," Annabelle suggested.

Sam put his napkin on his plate. "I'm starting to get a headache," he said to his dad.

"I'm with you, Sam the Man," his dad said. "Let's hit the road!"

The white minivan didn't exactly smell like a new car, Sam thought as he climbed into the backseat, but it did smell nice. It smelled like lemon dishwashing soap mixed with pine needles.

"I wonder what dragons smell like," Sam said to his dad. "Or *smelled* like, before they went extinct."

Sam's dad started the car. "I've got good news for you, Sam the Man. Dragons never went extinct."

Really? This was the best news Sam had gotten all day!

"Of course, that's because dragons never existed in the first place," Sam's dad continued. "Except in people's imaginations."

Sam hated of-courses. Of-courses always

went in front of bad news. But wait a minute. What did his dad just say? Sam thought about it.

"So if something exists in your imagination, it can never go extinct?" Sam asked his dad after he finished thinking.

"That's right, Sam the Man."

"So that's good news, right?"

His dad nodded. "I think so."

Sam thought so too. "Well, in my imagination dragons smell like fireplaces the day after you've burned a fire. Sort of smoky and cold."

"That sounds about right," Sam's dad said. "It's a good smell, but also a little sad."

"Yeah, dragons do smell a little sad," Sam agreed. "Maybe because people are scared of them. Maybe dragons are nicer than we think."

Sam liked having talks like this with his dad. His mom was nice to talk to too, but she was a lot more practical than his dad. His mom wanted to talk about whether or not it was time to get Sam new shoes or what kind of pie she should bake for Thanksgiving dinner at Grammy's house—apple or pumpkin. His dad liked to talk about stuff like if words had colors, what color each word would be.

Sam's dad just seemed more interested in the important stuff in life, Sam thought.

"So what exactly are you going to paint with this paint we're getting?" Sam's dad asked as they pulled into the shopping center parking lot. "You're not really thinking about painting the van, are you? Because first of all, that would take a whole lot of paint."

Sam took a deep breath. He let it out. Was it time to tell his dad the real plan?

"This paint is for something else," he said. "But I would like to paint the minivan, too. In fact, I would like to paint it to look like a dragon. It would be a monster minivan."

"Like a monster truck, only a van?" his dad asked.

Sam nodded, feeling excited. His dad understood his plan!

"That's a really cool idea, Sam the Man," his dad said.

Yes! His dad was going to say yes!

"Of course . . . ," his dad continued.

Sam felt his excitement disappear as soon as he heard "of course." He closed his eyes and waited for the bad news.

Sam's dad put his arm around Sam's

shoulder. "Of course, I don't think it's very practical."

Practical? Who cared about practical? Maybe Sam's mom did, but his dad understood about dragons and monster trucks. His dad was the least practical person Sam knew if he didn't count Gavin.

"I think it's very practical," Sam argued. "If you have a monster minivan painted like a dragon, it will scare bad guys away."

"But what if Mom needs to drive the van to an important meeting?" Sam's dad asked. "I'm not sure a monster minivan is the most professional-looking car in the world."

"Are you kidding me?" Sometimes Sam couldn't believe the things his dad said. "People respect dragons. Dragons are powerful. And they can fly."

"That's true," Sam's dad agreed. "So what's your vision for this dragon monster minivan, Sam? Help me see it."

"I'll show you the picture I drew of it when we get home," Sam said. "I think when you see it, you'll agree that I have a very good plan."

"You always have good plans, Sam the Man," his dad said. "I'm just not sure this one will work out."

Sam did his best to sound agreeable and mature. "Let's wait until you see the picture before we make any decisions, okay, Dad?"

His dad nodded. "Fair enough, Sam."

Sam patted his dad on the back. "Sounds like a plan."

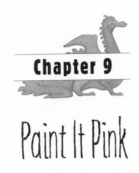

Chapter 9

Paint It Pink

"This is an awesome picture, Sam the Man," Sam's dad said when Sam showed him his drawing of a dragon monster minivan. "And you're right—our van would be the best minivan ever."

"And it would be very original," Sam pointed out. "I think being original is important, don't you?"

"It can be," Sam's dad said, handing Sam's picture back to him. "Sam, I don't

want to get your hopes up, but I do want to think about this. Maybe I can come up with my own plan. Will you give me until tomorrow?"

"Okay," Sam said. He could feel his hopes go up to the ceiling. His dad was practically saying yes!

It was seven fifteen. That meant Sam didn't have very much time to do his other plan, his bad news–good present plan for Annabelle. He went to his closet, pulled out his Hot Wheels suitcase, and put it on his bed. It had been a while since Sam had played with his cars. He guessed he'd gotten sort of tired of them, but now he wanted to take every car out and roll it around.

But Sam didn't have time for that. He plucked out his three monster trucks from the case. Okay, so which one would look best painted pink?

That was a question Sam never thought he'd have to ask.

He had the Prowler truck, the Pirate's Curse truck, and the Team Hot Wheels truck. The Team Hot Wheels truck was the most boring, so he decided it was the best one to paint.

Sam carefully spread out sheets of notebook paper across his desk. Then he took the tubes of red and white acrylic paint out of the bag. After he squeezed out a splotch of red paint onto the mixing plate and then squeezed a smaller white splotch next to it, he used a paintbrush to mix the two colors together. He could tell right away he was going to need to add more white paint.

He wished Miss Fran had been there to help him. He remembered what she said about glue, to do a little dab at a time, which seemed like good advice about paint, too.

Sam squeezed out a tiny blob of white and mixed it in. Better, but the paint was still too red. He squeezed out another tiny blob. Closer. Maybe two more tiny blobs would do it. He very carefully added a little more white paint and swirled it around. Perfect!

Now he wished Miss Fran were there so she could see what a great paint mixer he was.

Painting the truck would be trickier. He would have to be careful to not paint over the windows or get paint on the tires. (Although maybe it would look cool if the truck had pink tires? But if the tires had wet paint on them, how could he hold the truck to paint the other parts? Sam decided to leave the tires alone.)

The problem with painting a very small monster truck, Sam soon discovered, was holding it still while he painted. The tires might have been very small, but they still worked, and if Sam wasn't careful, the truck would flip around while he was trying to paint it.

The best thing to do, Sam decided, was to put the truck on his desk and hold the back tires with his thumb and middle finger while he painted the front of the truck and then hold the front tires while he painted the back of the truck.

He also decided putting small pieces of tape over the windows was a good idea.

Once he had figured everything out, it didn't take Sam that long to paint the truck. When he finished he still had fifteen minutes before it was time to give Annabelle her book back. The only question Sam had now was would the truck dry in time? Would blowing on it get it dry? Sam blew on it a couple of times

and then carefully touched it with the tip of his pointer finger.

His fingertip came back pink. Sam stood up and walked around his desk. He looked at the truck from the left, and he looked at the truck from the right. Pink wasn't Sam's favorite color, but he had to admit the truck was now amazing. If only it would hurry up and dry!

Sam needed a plan. He could try smudging the truck dry with a piece of toilet paper, but he thought that might be a bad plan. He could race it up and down the hallway and hope it got dry that way, but then Annabelle might come out of her room to see what was going on. Sam guessed he could turn on the blow-dryer to cover up the noise of the truck going up and down the hall.

The blow-dryer!

Suddenly Sam had an awesome truck-drying plan.

Sam got his rock collection shoebox from his closet and dumped all the rocks onto his bed. Very carefully, holding it by the front tires, Sam placed the very small pink monster truck into the box.

"I think you're going to enjoy this," he told the truck as he carried it to the bathroom.

If anyone asked Sam what he was doing with the blow-dryer, he'd just say he was fluffing up his hair for school in the morning.

The truck zoomed happily around the box as Sam chased it with the blow-dryer. Some of the paint rubbed off when the truck hit the sides, but Sam didn't think anyone would be able to tell.

Five minutes later the truck was completely dry. Sam pulled the tape off the windows and scraped a very small patch of pink paint from the left rear tire.

Now all he needed was a name.

The Annabelle Smasher? No, that sounded like Annabelle was getting smashed by the truck. The Annabelle Dozer, which sort of sounded like the Anna Bulldozer? No, because what it really sounded like was Annabelle was taking a nap. If the truck had been yellow, Sam could call it the Anna Banana, although he was pretty sure Annabelle didn't love that nickname.

Annabelle the Cannibal?

Cannonball Annabelle?

Cannonball Annie?

That was it! Cannonball Annie. When Sam was little, he used to call Annabelle "Annie," and Sam thought if he named the truck Annie, Annabelle might remember how Sam used to be little and cute, and maybe she would only get sort of mad at him instead of all the way mad at him.

It was worth a try.

Sam carried the shoebox with Cannonball Annie back to his room. He pulled a flat box out of his backpack. It was the box Miss Fran had given him after they'd finished working on Annabelle's book. Now all he had to do was return the book to Annabelle. Should he give her the truck first or the book first?

Truck, he decided as he carefully took the book out of the box. That way Annabelle would be in a good mood when he told her about the book.

But what if he didn't tell her about the book?

After all, if Cannonball Annie made

Annabelle happy, wouldn't telling her about the book just ruin her good mood?

Sam could always tell her about the book later, he thought. Annabelle probably wouldn't notice that there was anything different about the book, so why tell her right away? Sam had time, lots and lots of time, to break the bad news.

The Tell Annabelle Later plan.

Sam liked it.

The great thing about this plan was no one could be mad at him for not telling Annabelle. Sam was still going to tell her; he just wasn't going to tell her right that very second. In fact, if he waited a couple of weeks, Annabelle might have forgotten all about the book. "Oh, that old thing?" she might say. "I can barely remember what I wrote about, it's so unimportant to me now."

Yes, Sam thought, nodding to himself. That was an excellent plan.

Chapter 10

Your Own Personal Pink Monster Truck

Sam knocked on Annabelle's door. "It's me, Sam," he called.

"Come on in," Annabelle called back.

She was sitting on her bed with a drawing pad on her knees. "I'm working on a comic book about goats," she told Sam. "I figure if it gets published, Mom and Dad will have to let me get a goat for my lawn-mowing business."

Sam thought his sister was probably

wrong about that, but he didn't think it was a good time to say so. "I brought your book back, right on time," he told her. He was still standing in the doorway. "I'll go ahead and put it back in your trunk."

"What happened to it? Something's different about the yarn I used for the binding." When Sam didn't answer, she added, "Didn't it used to be purple?"

That's when Sam knew that the Tell Annabelle Later plan wasn't going to work. But maybe the Give Annabelle a Pink Monster Truck So She Won't Kill Me plan would.

"I have something for you," Sam said. He held out Cannonball Annie. "It's your own personal pink monster truck."

Annabelle reached out her hand and took the very small pink monster truck from Sam. "I've always wanted one of these."

Sam watched as his sister examined the truck. "I named it Cannonball Annie," he told her. "But you could change the name if you wanted. It's up to you."

"I like that name," Annabelle said. "And I like this truck. Thanks, Sam."

Sam's cheeks felt hot. He knew what he should do now, but he didn't want to do it. Maybe he could keep talking about the truck, explain how he mixed the paint until it turned the exact right shade of pink, or tell Annabelle about using the blow-dryer to get Cannonball Annie all the way dry. Maybe he could suggest that they have a monster truck race in the hall. He was pretty sure there was another blow-dryer in his mom's bathroom, so they could each blow-dry their trucks down the hallway. That sounded like a lot of fun to Sam.

Sam was still holding Annabelle's book. You could hardly tell the cover had gotten crinkled. The inside pages looked almost exactly the same as they had before Sam had shoved the book into his backpack this morning. He never thought that Annabelle would notice the yarn was red instead of purple. Who noticed yarn?

"Annabelle, I need to say something," Sam said.

"Okay," Annabelle said, rolling Annie up and down her arm. "Speak."

Remember how I used to call you Annie when I was little? Sam almost asked.

I've recently discovered that it takes less than five minutes to blow-dry a very small pink monster truck, he almost explained.

I think Dad's going to let me paint the minivan to look like a dragon, he almost told her.

"I messed up your book this morning," is what Sam actually said.

"How did you do that?" Annabelle was

still sitting on her bed. She started rolling Cannonball Annie across her bedspread.

Sam looked at his feet. "I took it to school."

"You're sort of whispering, Sam," Annabelle said. "I couldn't hear what you said."

Sam cleared his throat. He was still looking at his feet, but this time he spoke in a louder voice. "I took it to school, and I sort of smushed it putting it back into my backpack."

"Why did you take it to school?"

"For inspiration," Sam said. "I was working on a picture of a dragon monster minivan to show Mom and Dad so that they'd let me paint the new van."

"The used new van," Annabelle corrected him.

"I think it should be the new used van," Sam said.

"Maybe," Annabelle said. She didn't sound very mad. "So hand over the book and let me take a look."

Sam handed her the book.

"It looks fine to me," Annabelle said after a minute. "I guess the cover is a little crinkled."

"My art teacher, Miss Fran, helped me repair it," Sam explained. "If you have any other books that need repairing, I could probably do the job."

"Good to know," Annabelle said. "So did you paint this truck pink for me because you felt bad about the book?"

Sam nodded.

"Good plan, Sam," Annabelle said. "I like a present when I get bad news."

"I'm really sorry," Sam said, and he did feel sorry. But he also felt good that the bad news was out. "Thanks for not being supermad."

Annabelle started rolling Cannonball Annie across the top of her head. "Oh, I was really mad when I first heard about it, but I appreciate all the work you've done to repair the book and make me my own pink monster truck."

Sam took a step back. "What do you mean 'when you first heard'?"

"When Gavin called tonight when you and Dad were at the store. He asked me if I could see where the pages had gotten ripped in the book, and when I told him you hadn't given me the book back, he hung up."

"He said he could keep a secret!" Sam

cried out. "It's like first grade all over again!"

"Maybe he thought it wasn't a secret anymore," Annabelle said with a shrug. "I think he was just proud of you for fixing the book."

"I guess," Sam said. He still felt mad, but he felt less mad when he remembered that it was Gavin's idea to get Miss Fran's help fixing the book. That had been a good plan. Come to think of it, a lot of people had been coming up with good plans lately, Sam realized. Mrs. Kerner's idea to give Annabelle a present had been a good plan, and Mr. Stockfish and Miss Fran's idea to be honest about messing up Annabelle's book had been, he had to admit, a good plan too.

The only bad plan had been Sam's

plan to keep Annabelle from noticing that her book had gotten messed up. Well, it wasn't the worst plan—she really seemed to like Cannonball Annie. It just hadn't worked.

Sam wasn't used to his plans not working. But maybe that's because most of the time, he got help making his plans great. Speaking of which, he wondered what great idea his dad was going to come up with for the minivan.

"So me and Dad are going to turn the minivan into a fire-breathing dragon monster van," Sam told Annabelle, getting excited about it all over again. "It was my idea, but Dad's going to figure out the details."

"Does Mom know about this plan?" Annabelle asked.

"Not yet," Sam said. "I guess she'll hear about it tomorrow along with everybody else."

"It had better be a good plan," Annabelle said.

"A super-duper good plan," Sam agreed.

Chapter 11

The Fire-Breathing Dragon Monster Minivan Plan

At the breakfast table the next morning, Sam's dad didn't say anything about painting the minivan. Maybe he didn't have a plan yet, Sam thought. He decided to keep his mouth shut and not ask. Maybe his dad's plan was so massive that it would take all day to put together.

Maybe his dad had a friend who was a minivan painter, and as soon as Sam left for school, his dad would text his friend to come right over and start painting!

Sam got ready for school as fast as he could. He ate three spoonfuls of cereal, brushed his teeth a total of twelve seconds, and wore the same clothes he wore the day before so he wouldn't have to waste time picking out something new.

Gavin was already at the bus stop when Sam got there. Should Sam say something about Gavin spilling the big secret? Sam reminded himself that if Gavin hadn't told, Annabelle might not have gotten all her madness out of her system before Sam brought the book back.

So Sam decided to keep his mouth shut and not say a word, even when Gavin gave him twenty-five guilty looks on the way to school.

Sam also kept his mouth shut when Mr. Tiberis, his PE teacher, announced that because everyone was enjoying square dancing so much, he was extending the square-dancing unit for another week. He thought maybe if he kept a good attitude all day, his dad would have the minivan painted by the time Sam got home.

Sam was quiet all morning. Being quiet was the best way Sam knew how to have a good attitude. He was quiet when he got his subtraction homework back and saw three red x's on it, and he was quiet when he opened up his lunch and saw that his dad had mixed up the sandwiches, so instead of his usual peanut butter and jelly, Sam got Annabelle's turkey and avocado.

But when Mr. Pell sat everyone down

for after-lunch reading and pulled out *How to Train Your Dragon*, Sam just had to say something.

"My dad is painting our minivan right now, and it's going to be a dragon!" he told the class.

"A fire-breathing dragon?" asked Rashid.

"I'm pretty sure," Sam said. "Because otherwise it might get mistaken for a dinosaur."

"A velociraptor looks a lot like a dragon," Will agreed.

"Did you know someone discovered a new kind of dinosaur and called it *Dracorex hogwartsia?*" Emily asked. "It's named for Harry Potter, and it looks a lot like a dragon."

"Does that mean dragons are real?" Caitlyn asked.

"No," Emily said. "Dragons aren't real."

"Yes," said Hutch, Rashid, and Will all at the same time. "They're real!"

"They're real in your imagination," Sam said, feeling diplomatic. "And soon there will be a real fire-breathing dragon monster minivan in my driveway!"

"That's great news, Sam!" Mr. Pell said. "Maybe you could take a picture and e-mail it to me. I'll put it on our class website. But now it's read-aloud time."

"Everybody, be quiet!" Sam told his classmates. "Mr. Pell is going to read!"

Then he was quiet for the rest of the afternoon.

"Can I come over to your house to see the dragon monster minivan?" Gavin asked on the bus ride home. "Because I think it's probably the coolest thing I'll ever see in my entire life."

Sam was a hundred percent sure that when he got home, the dragon monster minivan would be sitting in his driveway.

Well, he was 99.9 percent sure.

Okay, 92 percent sure.

"How about I call you after I get home?" Sam asked Gavin. "It's sort of this special thing with me and my dad."

"It could be a special thing with you and your dad and me," Gavin said. "I could be like your adopted brother."

"I'll call you," Sam repeated.

"Okay," Gavin said.

As Sam got closer to his house, he started squinching his eyes. He wasn't sure why he was squinching his eyes until he got all the way to his driveway and knew he'd been squinching his eyes just in case there wasn't a fire-breathing dragon monster minivan in his driveway.

There wasn't a fire-breathing dragon monster minivan in his driveway.

There was just a plain white minivan with something stuck to the side right above the place where you put the gas in.

When Sam got closer he could see that the thing stuck to the minivan's side was a sticker, and when he got even closer, he could see that it was a dragon sticker. The dragon was a little kid's cartoon dragon, the kind that looked like it was made out of pillows and would like to hug you.

This was his dad's great plan?

A little-kid-hugging pillow dragon?

Sam stomped across the grass to the

front door, even though he was supposed to use the front walk.

He stomped into the house, down the hallway, into the kitchen, and over to the refrigerator.

He reached into the freezer and took out three waffles from the box, even though he was only supposed to eat two for his snack.

A cartoon dragon sticker?

That was the worst plan Sam had ever heard of.

"Sam the Man!"

Sam's dad walked into the kitchen. "I came home early this afternoon to get started on the minivan plan. You're not going to believe what I came up with!"

Sam took a chomp of frozen waffle and chewed. Hard. "You came up with a sticker," he said, his mouth still full. "I already saw it."

Sam's dad laughed. "The sticker was your mom's idea. I told her it was the wrong kind of dragon, but she thinks it's cute."

"Dragon monster minivans aren't

supposed to be cute," Sam said. He still felt mad, but he felt a little less mad now that he knew the sticker was his mom's idea and not his dad's.

"Listen, Sam the Man, I know you want this minivan to be a dragon van, but you have to be realistic."

Sam sat down at the kitchen table and took another bite of frozen waffle. It was never a good thing when grown-ups told you to be realistic.

"Think about it this way, Sam the Man," his dad sad, sitting down across from him. "What would you do if we were at the shopping center and you saw a dragon monster minivan in the parking lot?"

Sam thought about this for a minute while he chewed. "Well, I'd want to go over and look at it," he said after he swallowed. "And I'd probably want to hang out with it."

"Maybe climb on it?"

"Sure," Sam said. "I'd probably want to climb on it. Who wouldn't want to climb on a dragon?"

"So now imagine you're the person who owns the dragon monster minivan. Imagine what it would be like to pull out of a parking lot and realize there was a kid on top of your car."

"That wouldn't be good," Sam had to admit.

"No, it wouldn't," Sam's dad said. "And it wouldn't be good to have people touching your van all the time because then the paint would end up coming off, and you'd have to repaint it, and it would end up looking terrible because it's hard to get new paint that matches your old paint."

Sam started eating waffle number two. "So you're saying it would be a pain to have a fire-breathing dragon monster minivan."

"Not quite," Sam's dad said. "I'm saying it would be a pain to have the *outside* of your van be a fire-breathing dragon monster minivan."

"But not the inside?" Sam asked, feeling hopeful. "You mean we could paint the inside?"

"Not quite, but almost," his dad said. "Come look at my computer with me."

Sam followed his dad into the office. His dad clicked the computer mouse, and a picture appeared on the screen. Sam had to look at it a minute to realize what it was.

"Dragon scales?" he asked his dad. "Like real dragon scales?"

"Like real dragon scales from somebody's imagination," his dad said. "This person used their imagination to design dragon-scale fabric. That's what you're looking at."

"So we could make dragon-scale curtains for the minivan?" Sam asked. "Wouldn't that make it hard for the driver to see?"

"Not curtains—seat covers!" Sam's dad got a big grin on his face. "And we can get dragon-scale rugs, too. And you know how the back window has its own windshield wiper?"

Sam nodded. The back windshield wiper was his favorite one.

"I found a dragon-scale stick-on made

especially for windshield wipers! The minivan will look like it has a dragon's tail! So how's that for a plan, Sam the Man?"

Sam wasn't sure. It wasn't the worst plan. It wasn't even a bad plan.

But it wasn't exactly Sam's plan. And even though Sam knew that his plans were better when other people helped him with them, he wasn't sure this was the best plan for the van.

"I need some time to think about it," he told his dad.

And then he went to his room and sat at his desk and started to think.

Chapter 12

Sam the Man and the Minivan Plan

Sam thought about how even if the minivan looked like a dragon on the inside, it would still look boring on the outside.

He thought about how he'd told everyone in his class that he was going to have a fire-breathing dragon monster minivan.

He thought about the fact that dragons never existed.

He thought, What if minivans had never existed, but dragons had?

That was his favorite thought of all.

Sam pulled open his top desk drawer and took out the picture he'd drawn of the dragon monster minivan that lived in his imagination. Why were things that lived in Sam's imagination so much better than real things? Why didn't people paint their minivans to look like monster trucks? Why didn't they paint school buses to look like scary jack-o'-lanterns?

After a while, Sam got tired of thinking.

"I need to go take Mr. Stockfish for a walk," he told his dad as Sam put on his jacket and hat. "And I need to take care of the chickens."

Mr. Stockfish was waiting for him when Sam got to his house.

"You're seven minutes late," Mr. Stockfish said, looking at his watch. "Leroy is
getting hungry."

"But we don't have an official time,"
Sam said. "I always come over when I finish eating my waffles."

"Yes, and usually you're here seven
minutes ago," Mr. Stockfish complained as
they began to walk toward Mrs. Kerner's
house and the chicken coop. "Did you
decide to toast your waffles this time?"

"I never toast my waffles," said Sam.
"When you toast them, they turn brown. I
like my waffles yellow."

"That's ridiculous," Mr. Stockfish said.
"Waffles are supposed to be toasted to a
nice crisp brown and eaten with syrup or
whipped cream."

Sam didn't bother replying. They'd

already had this argument a hundred times.

It took a while to get to Mrs. Kerner's house because Mr. Stockfish had seen a TV show on squirrels the night before, and now he wanted to stop and look at every squirrel they saw on the way.

"Do you know that a squirrel's teeth never stop growing?" Mr. Stockfish asked Sam. "They have to gnaw on things to keep their teeth short."

"So what if a squirrel broke its jaw and couldn't gnaw?" Sam asked.

"Teeth five inches long," Mr. Stockfish said. "Maybe a foot."

"But it couldn't bite you because its jaw was broken," Sam pointed out. "So we wouldn't have to be scared of it."

"I have never been scared of a squirrel in my life," Mr. Stockfish said with a harrumph. "A raccoon, yes, but a squirrel? Never."

"It would be bad to be afraid of squirrels," Sam agreed. "Because they're everywhere."

"It's time to stop talking now," Mr. Stockfish said.

"Okay," said Sam.

They were only two mailboxes away from Mrs. Kerner's house when Sam heard a funny noise. It was a rumbling, grumbling, growling sort of noise. It was a big engine noise.

"Good grief!" Mr. Stockfish said. "What's making that racket?"

Three seconds later a big white truck drove past them.

It wasn't a monster truck, but it was

the biggest regular pickup truck Sam had ever seen. It had big tires and a big cab and a big bed.

And it had a big orange tiger painted on the side of the door.

"Wow!" Sam cried. "That's the coolest truck I've ever seen."

"That truck is ridiculous," Mr. Stockfish said. "Who would paint a tiger on their truck?"

"I would," Sam said, wondering who *wouldn't* paint a tiger on the side of their truck if they had permission to.

"You think you would *now*," Mr. Stockfish said as they turned and walked down Mrs. Kerner's driveway toward her backyard. "But wait until you're older."

"Didn't you want to paint something on your car when you were a kid?" Sam asked.

"We didn't have a car when I was young," Mr. Stockfish said. "We lived in the city and didn't need one. And, quite frankly, we couldn't afford one."

"Did you wish you had one?"

Mr. Stockfish was quiet for a moment. "It would have been nice," he said finally.

The chickens clucked and clacked when they saw Sam and Mr. Stockfish. Sam went into the coop to give them food and fresh water. When he was done, he carried Leroy over to Mr. Stockfish, who was sitting in his favorite lawn chair.

Sam sat down next to Mr. Stockfish and tried to imagine him as a little kid. But all he could imagine was a shorter version of Mr. Stockfish. He wondered if Mr. Stockfish the little kid had been as grumpy as Mr. Stockfish the grown-up.

He wondered if not having a car when he was a little kid was what turned Mr. Stockfish into a grumpy adult.

He wondered if he should quit making such a big deal about turning their plain old minivan into a fire-breathing dragon monster minivan.

"I almost forgot, Sam," Mr. Stockfish said after he gave Leroy a kiss on the top of her head. He dug his hand into his pocket and pulled something out. "I found this at the supermarket yesterday. I thought you might like it."

Mr. Stockfish had never given Sam a present before. "Thanks," Sam said. "What is it?"

"Take a look," Mr. Stockfish said, and opened up his hand.

He almost sounded happy.

◎ ◎ ◎

When Sam got home, he went into his dad's office. His dad was working on his computer. The screen was filled with rows of complicated-looking numbers that made Sam feel confused just seeing them.

"I was thinking that maybe we should do leopard-skin seat covers like Annabelle wanted," Sam told his dad. "And we could just keep the same rugs that came with the new used minivan."

"Or is it the used new minivan?" his dad asked, turning around to face Sam.

"Could we stop doing that now?" Sam asked his dad.

His dad nodded. "Yeah, I think it's time. But why the switch? Did you get tired of dragons?"

"I still like dragons," Sam said. "And

I still like monster trucks. But I guess our van is okay like it is. Except for that sticker Mom put on it. I really hate that sticker."

"Me too," Sam's dad agreed. "But it makes your mom happy."

"Does that mean we have to keep it?"

"I'm afraid it does, Sam the Man."

Sam sat down on a box of files across from his dad. "I've got another plan, if you want to hear it. It's sort of a mini-plan."

"I like all of your plans, Sam," his dad said. "Even the small ones."

Sam pulled out the present Mr. Stock-fish had given him. "I would like to stick this on the minivan's dashboard with a dab of glue so I can look at it whenever we go someplace and pretend I'm riding in a fire-breathing dragon monster minivan."

141

In Sam's hand sat a tiny dragon made out of plastic. It was one-inch long and a half-inch tall, with shimmery scales and a plastic red flame shooting out from its mouth.

"Do you think Mom would say it's okay?" he asked his dad.

Sam's dad smiled. "I think we can convince her. We'll ask her when she gets home."

"And then when we get the dragon stuck to the dashboard, can we take a picture for my class website?"

"Sure, Sam the Man," his dad said, turning back to his computer screen. "Are you guys studying dragons now?"

"No, school's never that perfect," Sam said with a sigh. "But we still have a lot of dragon fans in my class."

"And monster truck fans too, I bet," said Sam's dad.

"Monster *minivan* fans," corrected Sam, and then he took his real plastic mini–fire-breathing dragon upstairs to see if Annabelle would let it take a ride in her very small pink truck.

A monster in a monster truck. It sounded like a plan to Sam.

Acknowledgments

Thanks go to Caitlyn Dlouhy, who makes everything better with her magic green pen, and to her most accomplished accomplice, Alex Borbolla. Thanks to Justin Chanda, my favorite rooftop gardener and book publisher. Thank you, Amy Bates, for once again bringing Sam and his family to life through your illustrations. A big dose of gratitude goes out to copy editor Clare McGlade, who makes everything right. As always, many thanks and much love to my marvelous family—Clifton, Jack, Will, and Travis, the very good dog.

What will Sam plan next?
Find out in this sneak peek of

SAM THE MAN & the Secret Detective Club Plan!

Sam the Detective Man

Sam Graham was a mystery man.

Doing detective work had never been his plan, but when his sister lost her sock, Sam discovered he had a talent for figuring things out.

The sock had pink and purple stripes. Annabelle had looked for it under her bed and behind the dryer and inside her book bag, but the sock was nowhere to be found.

"Did you check your sock drawer?" Sam had asked when they discussed the case at the dinner table.

"Of course I checked my sock drawer," Annabelle said. "That was the first place I looked."

Sam thought about this for a moment. "Did you check every sock ball in your sock drawer? It was Dad's week to fold the laundry, and he always makes sock balls out of the socks."

"It's the best way to keep socks together," Sam's dad said.

Sam pointed a broccoli stalk at his dad. "But this week when you folded the laundry you were watching TV at the same time, right?"

"That's right," Sam's dad said. "The Monday-night football game was on. But what's that got to do with anything?"

"You always fold stuff in the same order," Sam explained. "Shirts, pants, T-shirts, underwear, socks. By the time you get to socks, I bet you're pretty bored."

Sam's dad shrugged. "Sure, I guess you could say that."

"Plus, you were pretty into the football game by then, am I right?" Sam asked.

"You are indeed right, Sam the Man," his dad replied.

"Okay," Sam said. "Here's my idea. You accidentally made a sock ball out of socks that didn't match. I bet if Annabelle went through her sock balls, she'd find her pink-and-purple–striped sock. You can only see the outside sock of a sock ball. The missing sock could be an inside sock."

"I'll go check," Annabelle said.

Two minutes later, she came downstairs waving a pink-and-purple–striped sock. "Sherlock Sam was right! Dad mixed up the socks."

Sam's dad smiled. "Very smart, Sam the Man. But what about the first sock—I mean the pink-and-purple–striped sock that wasn't lost? Why wasn't it in a mismatched sock ball too?"

"That's easy," Annabelle said, sitting back down at the table. "I never wash it. It's my lucky sock, and if I washed it, all of its good luck would get rinsed out."

"You never wash it?" Sam's mom asked. "As in *never ever*?"

"Never ever," Annabelle said. "I depend on that sock."

She turned to Sam. "You're a good detective. You should start your own

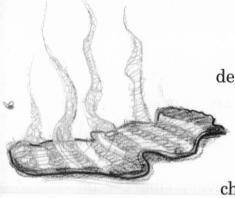

detective agency."

That sounded like a good plan to Sam. Maybe he could even charge money for solving mysteries. If he started a club for detectives, they could work on a lot of cases at once. That way they could make lots of money and also maybe get a little bit famous.

Sam liked the idea of being rich and a little bit famous.

Walking to the bus stop on Monday morning, Sam decided to ask his best friend, Gavin, about starting a detective club together.

"I don't know," Gavin said after they'd gotten on the bus and Sam had explained his plan. "I mean, I like the idea of being a detective. But finding missing socks doesn't sound very exciting to me."

"We'd work on bigger cases than that," Sam said. "Stuff like stolen diamonds and kidnapped cats. It'll be great."

"Kidnapped cats?" Gavin said. "When has anyone ever kidnapped a cat?"

Sam scrambled to come up with a better example of a mystery they could solve. "Okay, what about that time last year when someone stole Miss Fran's coffee cup and it was never found?"

Miss Fran was their art teacher. She'd been very sad about her missing coffee cup.

Gavin remembered. "Yeah, that cup had a picture of her dog on it. She was really upset."

"If we'd had a detective club, we could have cracked that case," Sam argued. "We could have saved Miss Fran's coffee cup!"

"I've always wanted to be in a club," Gavin said, and Sam could tell he was getting convinced. "That's the problem with second grade, in my opinion—there aren't any clubs. Well, unless you count the Clean Hands Before Lunch Club, which I don't."

"We could have other people in our club too," Sam said. "I think we need at least four people to be a real club."

Gavin thought about this. "But what kind of people? Some people I know would make terrible detectives. Like Morris Branch. Any time we have to take our shoes off for PE, he can never find them later."

"Or Rosie Schute," Sam added. "She

always gets lost from the group when we go on field trips. I think detectives should be able to find their group at the zoo."

"Okay, we need a list of what a good detective should be like," Gavin said, pulling a notebook and a pencil out of his backpack. "First of all, they should be good at figuring out clues."

Sam nodded. "And they should just— know stuff, I guess."

"They should be able to make good guesses!" Gavin said, writing in his notebook. "Guessing good is important. Also, they need to be good at writing things down."

"And asking questions," Sam said.

Gavin nodded. "That's a lot of stuff detectives need to be good at. So who do you think we should ask?"

"I'm not sure about everyone yet exactly," Sam said. "But I know who we should start with."

"Who?" Gavin asked.

"The smartest person in our class, of course," Sam said.

"That makes sense," Gavin said. "Are you thinking who I'm thinking?"

The bus pulled up in front of the school. Sam stood and picked up his backpack. "I bet I am," he said. "So let's go ask."

Meet the Chicken Squad:
Dirt, Sugar, Poppy, and Sweetie.

These **chicks** are *not* your typical barnyard puffs of fluff. . . . No, they're too busy solving mysteries and fighting crime. No mystery is too big or too small for the Chicken Squad—at least THEY don't think so.